THE ZERO DEGREE ZOMBIE ZONE

THE ZERO DEGREE ZOMBIE ZONE

PATRIK HENRY BASS

Illustrations by Jerry Craft

SCHOLASTIC INC.

No part of this publication may be reproduced, stored in a retrieval system, or transmitted in any form or by any means, electronic, mechanical, photocopying, recording, or otherwise, without written permission of the publisher. For information regarding permission, write to Scholastic Inc., Attention: Permissions Department, 557 Broadway, New York, NY 10012.

Library of Congress Cataloging-in-Publication Data Available

ISBN 978-0-545-13211-4

10 9 8 7 6 5 4 3 2 1   14 15 16 17 18

Printed in the U.S.A. 40
First paperback printing, September 2014

The text was set in Constantia.
Book design by Yaffa Jaskoll

To Mom and Dad,
for everything

Bakari Who?

I squeeze my eyes shut, then open them again. Shut, then open. Shut, then open. Nope, my name is still there. Finally I turn away. "Wardell, why did you do this to me?"

Wardell shrugs. He's my best friend — okay, pretty much my only friend — and half the time I still don't understand what goes on in that oversized melon he calls a head.

This is one of those times.

"I thought it'd be good for you," he mumbles.

"Good for me?" I can hear my voice going higher and higher. I sound more like my mom's ancient cat than a fourth-grade boy. I stab a finger at the piece of paper tacked onto Mrs. Crump's bulletin board.

There's my name under "Candidates for Hall Monitor."

And right below the only other name on the list. The only name that's ever been on this list, or any other list. Ever. In the entire history of Mrs. Crump's fourth-grade class at Thurgood Cleavon Wilson Elementary.

Until today.

"How," I ask Wardell, trying to get each word out, "is competing with Tariq Thomas good for me?"

I slowly glance across the room. There he is. Tariq Thomas. Thurgood Cleavon Wilson Elementary's golden boy. Tall, charming, athletic. Tariq has it all.

Including his own personal pep squad and enforcer rolled into one. Keisha Owens.

The very same Keisha who is currently glaring at me from beneath the tower of curls that makes her almost as tall as her cousin.

"What were you thinking, Bakari Katari Johnson?" Keisha demands. Her voice carries across the room with the might of a lioness. Heads turn to look at me, then back at her, then at me again. It's like a tennis match — and I'm the ball. "You go up against my cousin," she continues, "you're gonna get beat. You're gonna get beat hard!"

Tariq smirks. He doesn't say anything. He doesn't have to. Keisha says it all for him.

"Everybody knows Tariq's hall monitor," she warns me. "He's always been hall monitor, he will always be hall monitor. That's how it rolls here at Thurgood Cleavon Wilson Elementary. You can't get in the way of that. You do, you will get squashed." She slaps both hands together, then dusts them off like she's done with me. Only I know this is just the beginning.

"Well," Mrs. Crump announces with a smile, "I think it's nice that we have more than one candidate this time around." She looks at me with pity. "Good for you, Bakari, for giving it a try." Her eyes flicker to Tariq, and I feel like she just added, "Not that it'll do you any good."

Which is how I feel about it anyway. And why I'd never have signed myself up for hall monitor in the first place.

Thanks, Wardell.

"What were you thinking, dude?" I ask him through clenched teeth as I steer us away from the bulletin board and back to our seats. It's just about time to take roll. I push my glasses up on my nose. Mrs. Crump likes everyone in their seats, neat and prompt. "You know Tariq's gonna slay me."

"Maybe," Wardell agrees, squeezing his big bulk into

his chair. I swear, his head would look enormous on anyone else, but on him it actually looks small, like a cherry on a chocolate ice cream sundae. "But you don't know until you try." He shrugs again. "Just might surprise yourself."

That's one of the things I like about Wardell. Usually. He's always looking for the positives. "When life hands you lemons, make lemonade," as my wise granddad used to say. And Wardell sure likes his lemonade.

Times like this, though, I don't see exactly how lemonade's gonna help me much. With two candidates for hall monitor, Mrs. Crump's gonna let the class vote. She likes putting some things in the hands of the fourth-grade people in her class. And the people love Tariq.

Me?

Not so much.

Not that most of my classmates hate me. Least, not so far as I know. They just don't think much about me at all. Most of them probably don't even know my name.

Right now I have two votes: me and Wardell.

That's a landslide for Tariq.

Mrs. Crump starts calling roll, but I barely hear her. I'm too busy worrying about what's gonna happen come election time.

I reach into my pocket and find my granddad's lucky marble. It's a nice one, big as a quarter and pale gray, made of granite instead of glass. "That marble's magic," he'd say every time we played. "Pure magic. All you need in life, Bakari, is three things: light, courage, and power. You bring the courage and the will, this here marble will do the rest." He always had it in his hand or in his pocket, always. One day a month back, after he'd gotten real sick, he handed it to me. "Hang on to this for me, Bakari," he said. "And trust in the magic. Remember: light, courage, power." He died just a couple days later. Rolling that marble back and forth between my fingers makes it feel like

he's still here with me. But I'm not sure even he could help me out of this mess.

"Johnson, Bakari Katari," Mrs. Crump calls, and I raise my hand. At the same time, I hear Keisha say, "Who?" to Tariq, loud enough for most of the class to hear. A bunch of kids laugh. My stomach does a flip-flop. Great.

After attendance — and Tariq's resounding, "Yes, ma'am!" at his name — we get out our math books. My stomach's still banging around, and I feel like I might puke. The constant whispers and giggles between Keisha and Tariq — along with weird looks at me — aren't helping.

"Mrs. Crump?" I ask, holding up my hand. "Can I go to the bathroom?"

Mrs. Crump's okay — a little strict, but not mean — and I guess I look as bad as I feel because she takes one glance and nods. "Here, Bakari." She hands me the bathroom pass. "Not too long, okay?"

I nod and light out of there, but not before Keisha whispers, "You can run, but you can't hide, loser."

Her laughter follows me out.

Out in the hall I feel a little better. Especially once I can't hear Keisha laughing anymore. I know it's just nerves messing with me. That doesn't make them stop, though.

I head to the bathroom. Maybe some cold water will do the trick.

I'm halfway there when a blast of air hits me across the face. It's a warm early fall morning. Did somebody leave a freezer open somewhere?

Then a glowing, sharp blue disk appears out of thin air, floating about even with my head.

Whoosh!

A pair of arms shoots out of it, pale blue and cold as ice — and grab my shoulders.

Ouch!

The arms give me a hard yank, and I'm off my feet — and falling headfirst through that disk.

This day's just getting worse and worse!

2

Dialed Down to Zero

Y ou!"

The voice booming down at me is big and cold and about as friendly as a python. I glance up . . .

And up . . .

And up some more . . .

Until I'm practically falling over backward. And I'm already on my backside from when those hands dropped me. Onto an ice rink, feels like. My backside's going numb already. But I forget all that as I stare up at this mean stranger towering over me. He's gotta be seven feet easy. And his skin's so pale it's actually blue. He looks like he's been carved out of ice. And he's scowling fit to burst.

"Who, me?" I manage to squeak out, because his cold blue eyes are fixed on me and me alone.

"Yes, you," he bellows. "Bakari Katari Johnson. Return me my ring!" And a hand the size of my head reaches down, palm up, like I'm supposed to slap him a high five or something.

Only I have no idea what he's talking about.

"What ring?" I ask. I manage to get back on my feet, which I guess makes me feel better, 'cause questions start spilling out of my mouth. "And who're you? And where am I? And how'd you know my name?"

"I am Zenon," he answers. "I am the ruler of this place, the Zero Degree Zombie Zone." I get the "zero degree" part — I'm starting to shiver, and not just out of fright, and I think my nose just froze — but "zombie zone"? Then I actually look around for the first time.

Crap.

It's less like an ice rink than a scary winter wonderland, really. There's plenty of ups and downs, hills and valleys, and even what look like houses off a ways, but everything's made of ice, all blue and white. I'm in an ice village. Then there's the people. I thought this Zenon guy and I were alone because I didn't hear any loud noises. I guess it's because the rest of them don't talk much. Or maybe at all.

What they do is lumber about, arms out, eyes wide, mouths hanging open.

You know, like zombies.

Only made of ice. Or frozen, anyway. Zombie Popsicles. Zomb-sicles. Yuck.

Of course, even though I'm so scared I'm shaking — and so cold I'm shaking even more — my mind starts going a mile a minute. Like it does. I'm standing here with a zombie lord, NHL all-star interrogating me about some missing ring. All I can think about is: How'd this place get so cold? Where'd all these zombies come from? Were they already zombies, and then it got cold and they became zomb-sicles? Or were they just regular people and then it froze and turned them into zombies? Did this guy Zenon do that, or did he just happen along afterward and decide, "I kind of like it here, think I'll stay and make myself king of the place"? He's not clumsy and he can talk, so is he not a zombie? Or does being the zombie lord come with perks like keeping your brain and your tongue? Did he just have a better tolerance for the cold than the rest? Was he the only one smart enough to grab a jacket?

All these questions tumble through my head, but get interrupted midstream when Zenon stoops down to

glare at me eye to eye. Up close his eyes look like little blue gems, all sharp-edged and glittery under big, shaggy, white eyebrows.

"Are you listening to me, Bakari Katari Johnson?" he growls and his voice is that low quiet rumble you know means you're in serious trouble. My dad gets like that sometimes, and it's way worse than when he is mad, so I just gulp and nod.

"Uh, yes, sir, Mr. Zenon, sir," I answer after a second.

"Good." His lips are even bluer than the rest of his skin, and they curve up just a little, almost like a smile. Almost. "Then where is my ring?"

Gulp. "I don't know anything about a ring," I tell him. "Honest."

"No?" Now he's frowning at me. Great. Like I'm not scared enough as it is. "And yet I heard your name when my ring disappeared. Why is that?"

"Uh, maybe it just sounded like my name?" Uh-huh, because "Bakari Katari Johnson" is so easily mistaken for "Tariq Thomas" or whatever. Sure.

He's not buying it, either. "What have you done with my ring, Bakari Katari Johnson?" Dude, I wish he'd stop reciting my full name every time he asks me a question. I feel like I'm in the principal's office or something. If the principal shot up two feet and turned into a walking ice sculpture, that is.

"I don't have it! Really!" I start turning out my pockets. "Look!" Half a stick of gum pops out — thanks, Wardell. Then there's a rubber band, a little stub of a pencil, two quarters, a finger puppet, a Kleenex, and Granddad's marble. "See? No ring!"

Zenon frowns and pokes at the little pile. My heart almost stops when his finger lands on the marble, rolling it back and forth, but then he moves on and I breathe again. Unfortunately, proving I don't have his ring doesn't convince him I'm not to blame. "You hid it" is what he says when he's done looking.

"I didn't hide it," I insist, stuffing everything back into my pockets. "I never had it! I don't even know what it looks like!"

He's not listening, though. Why are grown-ups always like that? Once they get an idea in their head they just won't listen to reason, or facts, or anything else. You can tell the truth — and they still won't hear you.

Just like now. "You have until the end of the day to return my ring, Bakari Katari Johnson," Zenon informs me, straightening up again. "If you do not deliver it, I will unleash my zombies upon your world and turn it into a frozen wasteland like my own!"

Great, no pressure.

"How am I supposed to give you your ring back when I didn't take it in the first place?" I ask, but Zenon just waves that off. "And how am I even supposed to get it to you?" I look around at all the zombies and the frozen landscape. "For that matter, how do I get back to Mrs. Crump's class?"

He waves again, but this time in a big circle, and where his hand cuts through the icy air a glowing blue line follows, like he's highlighting something. When his hand

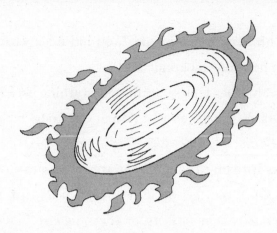

has gone full circle there's a glowing disk in the air, just like the one I got pulled through on my way to the bathroom. Zenon grabs it by one edge like it's a Hula-Hoop and tosses it toward me. "End of the day," he warns as it lands over my head and shoulders and glides down to the ground. "That is all the time you have, Bakari Katari Johnson. Do not delay, or your world will suffer the consequences."

"That's so not fair," I start to say back, but it's too late. The minute the disk settles around my feet, I feel warm air, and everything blurs. And then I'm standing in the hall of Thurgood Cleavon Wilson Elementary again.

I'd think I imagined the whole thing except there's a ring of melting ice at my feet, and my jeans are still frozen in places. Plus, my eyelashes are dripping.

Okay, so now on top of the whole hall monitor situation, I've got a crazy ice zombie lord telling me I need to give him back a ring I don't have or he's gonna let his ice zombies loose on the world.

I turn and slide back toward class. Even studying fractions is better than this!

3

Ring-a-Ding-Ding

Bakari, what happened to you?" Wardell asks me as soon as I take my seat again. "You look like the bathroom sink got up and took a swing at you." He flicks a drop of water off my sleeve. "You know you're supposed to wash in it, not swim in it, right?"

"Ha-ha, you're hilarious," I tell him out of the side of my mouth. We've got our math books open so we can follow along as Mrs. Crump explains a problem up on the board, and as long as we keep our conversation low and our eyes forward, we can still talk.

"But really, what happened?" I see him glance over at Keisha and Tariq. "I know it wasn't them, 'cause they haven't moved since you left."

I can't help it — I look over there myself. Of course, both of them are staring right at me. Great.

"No, it wasn't them," I admit. "It was even worse, if you can believe it."

"Worse? What, did Moses Allen decide to dunk you or something?" Moses is a fifth-grade legend, already as big as a truck. I've heard that he got held back a grade, maybe even two, but he'd be big even for a kid in junior high. Heck, he's big for an NBA player! Fortunately, he's not that bad — he throws his weight around a little, but he's not mean, you just have to stay out of his way if he's in a bad mood. Not like Keisha — I picture if she were Moses's size, and shudder. Talk about a nightmare!

"Naw, not him, either." For a second I think about coming up with some story, but I shake that idea off. This is Wardell we're talking about. He and I've been best friends since second grade, when we got stuck in a photo booth together on a field trip. This is the guy I tell everything to. The one person besides my parents who knows about my granddad, what he meant to me, how I cried at his funeral. This is the guy who'd share his last cheese stick with me — and Wardell loves his cheese sticks.

So instead I tell him the truth.

"You're not gonna believe this," I start, but I shouldn't have worried. In addition to looking on the bright side, Wardell's really good at believing. Yeah, so he's a little gullible, and it's gotten him into trouble before. It's really easy to play practical jokes on him. But right now I'm really glad that he's so agreeable about everything. I don't know what I'd do if I told him and he just laughed it off.

"Wow," he says instead when I'm done. "Are you serious? A whole world full of zombies? And they're all frozen and stuff? That's wicked!"

"It was wicked, all right," I agree. "Wicked cold and wicked scary."

"And you really don't have this ring that Zero guy wanted?"

"Zenon," I correct him. "And no, I really don't. I don't even know what ring he's talking about."

"But he's blaming you anyway." Wardell sighs. "Ain't that always the way?" He's got two brothers, an older one and a younger one, and he's always getting blamed whenever anything breaks or spills or whatever. Sometimes I hate being an only child, but when I look at Wardell and his brothers I think maybe it isn't so bad.

"All I know is —" I start, but then something hits me in the back of the head. What the —

I pick up the ball of paper and uncrumple it, smoothing it out on my math book. It says, "YOU'RE A LITTLE LOSER BOY" in big letters. I don't even need to glance over to know who wrote and threw this. Keisha.

"You're going down, lame brain!" she whispers, pointing one long tiger-striped fingernail at me. "You whisper all the strategies you want, you still ain't got what it takes to beat Tariq."

"Can't beat Tariq," Tariq chimes in happily, nodding along like it's got a beat to it. Sad thing is, it kinda does.

"Yeah, right!" I reply. Lame, I know. I've always got tons of good comebacks right on the tip of my tongue — until I actually have to say them, and then they all disappear into thin air. Instead I wind up saying something lame, or not saying anything at all, and looking even more like an idiot than I did before.

"'Yeah, right?' That the best you can do?" Keisha snorts. "Please, my baby brother's got more lip than that, and he's barely two!"

"Start feeling the heat, can't beat Tariq!" her cousin offers, grinning like he's just said something really deep.

Yay, so you can rhyme, I do it all the time, I think. But of course I can't manage to say it, and his smile just gets wider.

"Lay off me, Keisha," I tell her, and the way she's grinning you'd think she was a big old cat and I was a wounded bird that just fluttered down in front of her. "What's so funny?"

"You," she says through that smirk. "You're funny. You're in so deep, and down so bad, you don't even know it. You just keep talking and acting like it's nothing, but I can hear your knees shaking from here."

"I'm not scared of you or Tariq," I tell her, slamming my math book shut and standing to face her.

Big mistake.

"Bakari, is there a problem?" Of course Mrs. Crump heard my book closing and looked back — and now here I am, out of my seat, my book shut on my desk. While Keisha and Tariq have their heads bent over their textbooks like good little students.

"Bakari was saying something under his breath," Keisha reports, looking up like it's the first time. "I didn't hear what, exactly, but it looked like he was getting all worked up about something. Then he just slammed his book and jumped up from his seat." Her eyebrows raise, and her mouth forms a little O of surprise — or sympathy. "Are you okay, Bakari?" Then a little smirk flickers over her face. "How are your knees?"

"I'm good," I tell her, as sharp as I can. Then I turn back to Mrs. Crump. "I'm fine, ma'am, thank you. Just something poked my leg and startled me. It was probably my pencil, or maybe there's a rough spot under my desk." I rub at my leg to emphasize it. "I didn't mean to interrupt."

Mrs. Crump studies me for a second, then nods slowly. "Yes, well, return to your seat, please. Thank you. Now, where were we?"

Somebody — Faronda, I think — calls out the page number, and we return to the exciting world of integers and rays and diameters. Whew!

I toss an angry stare toward Keisha and Tariq and scowl as she turns away, concentrating.

And that's when I see it.

There's a ring on Keisha's left thumb. A big, heavy ring I've never seen her wear before. It's blocky and rough, like whoever made it didn't have proper training or tools or something. It's blue, or at least bluish, though from here it looks like there's some white and silver as well.

It looks like it could've been carved from ice.

"That's it," I mutter to myself. "That's the ring!"

"The ring?" It takes Wardell a second to catch up. "Hold on, you mean that Zenon guy's ring? The one you need to give him to stop a real-life zombie invasion? Let's get to it, then!"

"Yeah? How, exactly?" I look at him, then at Keisha and Tariq, then at Mrs. Crump. Too much distance between me and Keisha, and not enough between us and Mrs. Crump. There isn't a lot I can do from here.

Wardell's getting that, too, but he just shrugs. "So get in closer," he offers.

Again, a lot easier said than done. I have no idea how Keisha wound up with that ring, but it doesn't look like she wants to get rid of it any time soon. Not to mention she's about the last person I want to be anywhere near.

And just how did she get that ring?

4

Pileup for Four . . . Hold the Soup!

I try to lose myself in fractions. But between this whole ring thing and the hall monitor stuff, I'm having a hard time concentrating. When the lunch bell rings I think it's about the sweetest sound I ever heard.

"All right, class, line up for lunch!" Mrs. Crump calls out. There's a mass of usual noise as everyone slams their books shut, tosses them back inside their desks, scrapes their chairs back, and stampedes toward the door. "Nice neat lines!" she reminds us, just like a normal day, and we slow down and break into lines, boys and girls. Tariq's line leader for the boys, of course. Keisha's line leader for the girls, of course. They take their places right by the door, heads up like they're royalty or something, and everyone pushes and shoves to get as close behind them as possible.

Except for me. I hang back near the end of the line, Wardell right behind me. No sense asking for extra trouble.

Not that it helps any, of course. "Off to the lunchroom, on the double," Mrs. Crump tells us, opening the door and ushering us out, but she doesn't go with us. She never does. Most of the teachers eat at their desks, or in the teacher's lounge, with one or two keeping an eye on the cafeteria alongside the actual lunch ladies. Mrs. Crump isn't one of them. Wardell said that he heard from Moses that Mrs. Crump stops off at the teacher's lounge, then sits at her desk. I bet she sighs with relief the minute we're out of sight and she can read a magazine or eat a doughnut or whatever it is teachers do when their students are gone.

Unfortunately, that also means we don't have an adult with us between the classroom and the cafeteria. Which is why Keisha and Tariq can let most of the class rush past them down the hall and linger to tease me with no one around to stop them.

And that's exactly what they do.

"Ready to give up?" Keisha says, getting right up in my face. She's a bit shorter than I am, not counting all that hair, but she pops up on her tippy-toes so her eyes are

even with mine. "You ain't gonna win, so you might as well save yourself some humiliation and quit now."

I just stare back at her, until I realize she's actually expecting a reply. "Uh, I can't," I finally manage to mutter, my fingers going to Granddad's marble for strength and support. "Sorry."

"Sorry?" she practically screeches at me. "Sorry? Oh, you're gonna be sorry, all right!" Her tone goes soft and her scowl changes to a smile. For a second she's almost nice. "Come on, Bakari, why're you doing this? Everybody knows Tariq's gonna mop the floor with you." Tariq, who's been standing back out of the way and letting his cousin do all the talking — like usual — nods. It's his smug, matter-of-fact face, like, "Yep, you know she's right, nothing you can do about it." Tariq isn't even a bully. He just assumes he should get everything he wants, and ignores anyone who tells him otherwise. And of course he's got Keisha around to make it all happen.

She's still talking at me, still in super-friendly mode like we're cool. She says, "There's really no reason to go through all of this, is there? You can just concede the race, take your name off the sign-up sheet, and that'll be that. Tariq gets to be hall monitor again, and you" — she actually reaches up and pats my hair like my great-aunt Florence — "you get to go back to your nice, quiet life again."

Which sounds good, honestly. I didn't want to be hall monitor in the first place, and I still don't. Besides, I've got this whole zombie thing to figure out. I'd be happy to surrender the hall monitor race and let Tariq have it.

The only problem is, I can't.

See, conceding means I actually have to do something. And doing things isn't really my specialty. I'm an ideas guy, always thinking, always asking questions (at least in my head), always trying to figure stuff out, always imagining.

The actual doing? Not so much.

I tend to freeze up when I have to make decisions. Always have. So with Keisha telling me I should quit — I'd like to, I really would. But I can't. It's actually easier for me to keep going and to lose the election than it is for me to step out of the race right now.

Which, I know, is pretty lame of me. I know that. There just isn't much I can do about it.

That's why I wind up shaking my head to Keisha's offer.

Which is why she shoves me.

"Dumb move, little loser boy!" Her nicey-nice face vanishes in an instant, like somebody just scrubbed it away, and there's her normal Keisha glare in its place. "You gonna get ground beneath Tariq's heel!" And she shoves me a second time, hard, with both hands.

It's pure reflex that I reach out with my free hand — the one not clutching Granddad's marble — and grab her arm as I stumble and fall.

Which means she falls right on top of me.

And, since Tariq is directly behind me at the moment, when I fall backward I slam into him, and he topples over as well.

Wardell falls with us. I'm not entirely sure how, since he was behind Keisha and she fell toward me and away from him. But then it's Wardell. He's entirely capable of tripping himself by accident. All alone. While sitting down. No joke, I've seen it happen.

Anyway, there we all are on the floor, all four of us. There's a lot of pushing and shoving and elbowing going on as we each try to get free and get some space and stand back up.

It shouldn't surprise anyone that Tariq is the first back on his feet.

I happen to be next, which is a surprise, even to me.

Then Keisha pops up like a jack-in-the-box, bouncing and swaying and getting in my face again. "You think you can just knock me down?" she practically spits. "Yeah? Is that what you think?"

"You pushed me," I point out, but she's not hearing any of that. She's too busy waving her hand in my face, her bare fingers flicking back and forth before my eyes.

Wait a second — bare fingers?

I look again. Yep, five fingers, nothing but skin up to the paint-and-jewel-encrusted nails.

What happened to the ring?

I look around, checking the floor right where we were — and there it is, a glint of ice off to one side by some lockers, like some kid dropped an ice cube on his way to class. Only I know better. I hurry over and scoop it up. It's a lot heavier than it looks, a lot heavier than any normal ice, and it's freezing, numbing my fingers just from holding it. Keisha is so full of heat it's a wonder she didn't melt this ring, but, hey, I've got it! Once I figure out how to get it back to Zenon I can return it and the world won't have to worry about an ice zombie invasion. Hooray!

I drop the ring into my pocket — and freeze.

Because there wasn't a clink.

And ice colliding with Granddad's marble should have made a loud clink.

I shove my hand back into my pocket, but other than the ring, the rubber band, and the finger puppet, there's nothing there.

Nothing.

It can't have gone far, I tell myself quickly, frantically searching the area. It has to be — aha! Something catches the light across the hall, next to another locker. Something light-colored, gray maybe, and possibly round.

Yes!

Just as I'm starting toward it, though, Keisha gets in my way again. "I should get you written up," she snaps, "pushing a girl like that. What's the matter with you?"

"What? I didn't push you — you pushed me." I go to step past her, and she slides over to block me again. "Look, I won't say anything," I promise, "if you just get out of my way and leave me alone." I catch Wardell's eye and then glance over toward the marble. Come on, best friend, figure out what I'm trying to tell you, I think furiously.

I almost leap toward the sky when he looks over, sees the marble, starts, then glances back at me and nods. And ambles in that direction.

Yes!

And then Tariq sidles right past him, just slips by Wardell like he's moving in slow motion — which, admittedly, he sort of is — and crouches down to pick up the small, shiny thing that's captured our attention.

"A marble," Tariq says, holding it up to see it more clearly. "Sweet."

"Tariq —" I start as he straightens up, clutching my marble in one big hand. But I'm rudely interrupted. Again.

"Don't even try it," Keisha warns me. "Anything you gotta say to him, you can say to me."

"I need —" I try again, but she cuts me off.

"*You* need?" she snorts in my face. "What you need don't enter into it! It's all about what *we* need. And right now" — she flips her head, making her tall hair wave dangerously, before turning her back on me — "what we need is lunch."

She stomps off, Tariq right behind her, still admiring his new find. Leaving me and Wardell out in the hall, alone.

"Sorry," he tells me once they're gone. "I saw it on the ground and went for it, but Tariq was faster."

"I know." I sigh. "Well, at least I got this." I hold up the ring. It catches the light from the side windows almost like a prism, sending a cascade of color across the far wall. "Now I just need to figure out how to get it back to Zenon and it's all good."

Except I can't help but feel like that isn't going to work. Like without that marble I've got problems I don't even know about yet. Like trading it for the ring was a bad trade all around, but especially for me.

I need to get that marble back.

I just wish I knew how.

"Come on, before all the good brownies are gone," Wardell begs, grabbing my arm and dragging me toward the cafeteria. "We can figure out how to get the marble back and return the ring to that Zero guy after lunch."

"Yeah, I guess." I hang my head. I am sort of hungry under all the shaking in my body. "Let's go."

Maybe, I think as we start down the hall again, I can convince Tariq to trade me the marble for something else.

I wonder how he feels about string cheese.

5

A Little Undead Appetizer

Hey, you gonna eat that?"

I glance up from playing with my cold fish stick. Wardell's already got three crammed into his mouth and two more clutched in one hand, but he's still eyeing mine.

"Nah, go for it." I push the lunch tray toward him.

"Sweet, thanks!" He immediately grabs up the rest of my food. Fine by me. I'm not feeling real hungry anyway. I nibbled what I could, but between the hall monitor thing, the zombie and ring thing, and now the marble thing, most of my appetite is shot. I do manage to keep a death grip on my brownie, though, and ignore Wardell's puppy-dog eyes. It's not like he hasn't had two already!

"Dude, I gotta get that marble back," I tell him for the hundredth time. Tariq and Keisha are sitting on the other end of the fourth-grade table, surrounded by half our class, telling stories and laughing like this is the best party ever. Tariq's not even holding the marble, near as I can tell — looks like he's got a brownie in the hand he's waving around, and a bottle of juice in the other. I bet he just looked at Granddad's marble for a few seconds, then stuck it in his coat pocket and forgot about it. Or maybe he got bored and tossed it — my heart seizes for a second, but I don't really buy that one. He'd hold on to it, just in case he wanted it later. Besides, it's shiny, and Tariq likes shiny things, like gold medals.

"Whuddygonnado?" That's the best Wardell can manage around his mouthful of food. Good thing I'm sitting across from him — the spray doesn't quite make it to my side of the table.

I take a bite of brownie. "I wish I knew."

I'm just swallowing the bite when the cafeteria doors slam open — and two long shadows stretch all the way across the room.

I glance over, and my heart about stops again.

The two standing in the doorway are definitely not elementary school students — not unless we've got some new exchange program for giants that nobody told me

about. They've got to be over seven feet tall, their heads nearly scraping the door frame above them. They're not teachers, either. Not unless teachers are now going around wearing old rags that were probably clothes once, maybe a decade ago.

And then there's the whole blue-white skin thing. And the glazed-over, milky eyes. And the slack jaws. And the arms out, hands vaguely grasping air as they shamble into the room.

Uh-oh! Ice zombies! A pair of them, from Zenon's Zero Degree Zombie Zone.

But what're they doing here?

Ice zombies like brownies?

Really, it's no surprise at all that the first people to react are Tariq and Keisha. "Hi, can we help you?" Keisha asks in her fake, "Hello grown-up, I'm incredibly sweet and polite" voice as she bounces over. Tariq's right behind her, though I can see he's frowning as he eyes the frozen pair.

The ice zombies look down at them — not a lot of people in this school can look down on Tariq like that, and I have to admit I sort of enjoy it — and the one on the left opens his mouth. His teeth, amazingly, are perfect, and sparkle like, well, ice.

"Urrr!" he groans. And takes a single lurching step toward Keisha.

She backs up. "Sir?" she tries again. "Are you all right? Do you need some help? Are you feeling sick? Did you want to sit down?" She elbows her cousin, who finally says something.

"Yo, man, you want some juice or something?" Thank you, Tariq, that was very deep.

"Gaaah!" the one on the right replies. And stumbles toward Tariq. Who backsteps fast. I think he shivers a little, too, but I can't be sure from here.

"Maybe we should get the school nurse," Keisha offers. The zombie on the left reaches for her, but she sidesteps easily. "You really don't look good."

"Raaah!" he replies, trying for her again. I think all her politeness has turned him off. He opens his mouth wide, his teeth gleaming, and then he lunges, trying to bite down on her shoulder or arm.

"Hey!" All that fake politeness vanishes like she threw a switch — I still don't know how she does that. "What was that, salmon breath?" she snaps instead. Ah, the real Keisha has returned. "You just try to take a bite out of me? I don't think so!"

The other one goes for Tariq, who easily evades the ice zombie's clumsy attempts. "What's up with that?" I hear him mutter. "Dude's like ice. And bitey!"

I don't want to get involved — let Keisha and Tariq handle it, it's their school — but somehow I find myself clambering to my feet anyway. "You shouldn't be here!" I shout as I hurry over toward the ice zombies. Yes, a part of my brain is screaming at me, wondering what the heck I'm doing. There's a pair of ice zombies in my school, right in the cafeteria, and I'm walking toward them? What's wrong with this picture?

But I keep going anyway, stopping when I'm only a few feet away. Just out of their range. I hope. "You don't belong here," I tell them. "This place isn't for you." Then I lean in a little. "Look, I've got the ring," I say quietly. "Go back and tell Zenon I've got it. I can bring it to him as soon as we're done with lunch, okay?" I don't bring it out and wave it in their faces — that just seems really lame, the kind of dumb stuff people do all the time in the movies — but they should be able to figure out what I mean.

Except the way they're still looking at me, I'm not sure they can figure out much past "dinner" and maybe "lunch."

And "snack."

"Grrrrrr." The guy on the left snarls, and swings for me. He misses by a mile, bumping into one of the recycling bins instead. It goes flying, empty cans and water bottles and yogurt containers spilling out all over the floor. Guess they're not too worried about saving the planet where he's from.

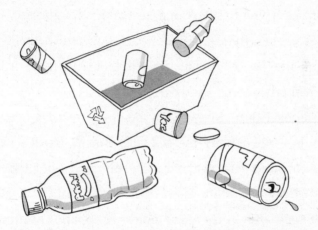

"Yaaaa," the one on the right adds, and grabs the nearest table. Kids scatter, pulling their legs and backpacks clear just before he flips the long table, seats and all.

That's what sets off the panic. There's fourth graders running everywhere, shouting and screaming.

Only problem is, there's only three ways out of our cafeteria. First, there's the sliding wall that blocks us off from the sections for the other grades. It's locked down tight, has been ever since a couple of kids took over the controls on their section a few years back and made the wall shimmy back and forth a dozen or so times, exciting everyone on both sides.

Then there's the door to the kitchens, which you can't open from our side without a key — the lunch ladies don't want us trying to sneak in and steal food, I guess.

And then there's the door back out into the hall. The same one the ice zombies are still blocking, more or less.

Nobody's going anywhere.

"Look I don't know who you think you are," Keisha shouts, "but nobody messes with Keisha Marie Owens like this and gets away with it. You move your fool self out of my way right now!" For once, though, Keisha's met her match — the ice zombies are apparently immune to her particular brand of scary charm, and her threat doesn't budge them one inch.

Then she makes the mistake of kicking one in the shin. "Ow!" she cries, hopping on her other foot while trying to massage the one she kicked him with. "What're you, made of stone? Broke my darn foot, you freak!"

Ice, actually, I think, but I don't bother saying it. What would be the point?

Tariq leaps in just then, glaring at the ice zombie. "Nobody messes with my cousin!" he shouts, and hurls himself at the monster, shoulder first like this is football and he's blocking for the QB. Too bad Mr. Ice Zombie towers over him by at least a foot and is frozen solid besides. Wow. For the first time in history Tariq fails at something. I probably shouldn't enjoy that as much as I do.

Especially since the one on the right has spotted me again, and starts making his way toward me, tossing tables and benches and food trays and trash cans aside as he goes. Any kid who gets too close to his flailing arms goes flying as well, but those milky eyes stay fixed on me. I think.

Gulp.

Maybe they understood about the ring after all.

There's got to be a way to send these guys back home. I reach into my pocket for Granddad's marble, hoping maybe he was right about it having magic — but of course it isn't there.

Instead my hand touches something squared off and heavy and really cold.

Oh, right.

I slide the ring onto my thumb and pull my hand out of my pocket, holding the ring up high. "Uh, I command you to go back to your own world!" I shout, trying to make myself heard over the crowd.

Nothing happens.

"Go away!" I try again, waving the ring in their direction.

Still nothing, other than my thumb going a little numb.

"Come on!" I shout, shaking the ring back and forth. "Do something, already!"

You ever have that feeling when you bite into something cold — really cold — and it's like the cold lances right through your brain?

I get a sensation just like that. Ow! Only it doesn't fade right away. And somehow, don't ask me how, I know it's coming from the ring.

"Yeah?" I mutter to it. "You think that's gonna stop me from using you? Guess again, chump. Bakari Katari Johnson is on the case, and you are gonna help me get these ice suckers home. Somehow."

The sharp pain continues, and I concentrate on it as hard as I can. Work!

I'm so busy tussling with this pain in my head, I almost

don't see it. But then out of the corner of my eye I glimpse something small, bright, blue, and glowing. I glance over, and it's a circle like the one Zenon sent me through. Yes!

Only it's about the size of a hamster wheel.

That's just not gonna do the trick.

"Grow!" I tell it through clenched teeth. The pain isn't going away, but I focus on it, using it to keep me on task. I've got the ring gripped tight in one hand, and I keep the pressure on mentally as much as I can. Too bad I'm more a relaxed kind of guy. Mental pressure isn't really my strong suit.

Still, I don't give up. And slowly the disk grows a little bigger. Now it's about the size of a soccer ball.

"You will do what I tell you!" I whisper to the ring. I'm squeezing it so hard it's digging into my skin, and there're dull flashes of pain radiating up from that spot in time with the sharp needle stabbing into my head, but I tell myself to stay strong and flash right back at it.

Now the hole's like a Hula-Hoop. Almost there!

The only problem is, the two ice zombies are halfway across the room from each other now — the one on the left is terrorizing kids near the kitchen door, while the one on the right hasn't strayed far from the hall door. They're keeping us boxed in, and making it impossible for me to do anything to both of them at once. It doesn't look like anybody's actually been bitten yet. Maybe they're not big on the taste of fourth graders? Maybe we're not quite ripe? But that's probably only a matter of time.

Unless I can get them moving.

"Hey, gross ice face!" I shout at the one by the kitchen. "You always look like this, or did somebody break a whole mess of ugly ice sticks over your head?"

He turns slowly, those filmy eyes sweeping around until finally they land on me. "Yeah, that's right," I tell him. "I'm talking to you. I don't see anybody else here looks like a frozen road accident."

He bares his teeth at me — not a pretty sight, no matter how sparkly they are — and starts staggering in my direction.

One down.

The pain makes me glance over at the disk again, and it's now taller than I am. Sweet.

· Time for number two.

"Yo, ice queen!" I call to the one by the hall door. "Yeah, you. I guess he's the ugly one, so you must be the stupid one, right? Do you even know what that means? Or is what little brain you once had completely frozen over?"

Now it's his turn to scowl at me and lumber after me as I move toward the center of the room, and closer to that glowing disk that I can still feel throbbing in my head and my hand.

Perfect.

I try not to think about what an incredibly bad idea this is.

"That's the best you two can do?" I ask instead, directing my words at both of them with my best Keisha-like sneer. "Really? I've got Popsicles at home scarier than you two."

They speed up a little. Not a lot, but probably as much as they can. I just hope it's fast enough, because I don't know how long I can hold this disk open.

"Oh, please!" I shout when they're each maybe four feet from me. My head's splitting, but the disk is as tall as they are now, and twice as wide. And I'm standing right beside it. "I'm right here!" I tell both ice zombies. "Come and get me! Can you even get that right?"

That does the trick. They both growl like hungry dogs and break into clumsy runs, arms out, mouths open, moaning and gurgling.

And I step out of the way just in time for both of them to crash into the disk from opposite sides.

But instead of colliding in the middle, they both charge through it — and vanish.

The second they're gone I stop thinking about the stabbing cold, letting go with a shudder. The disk disappears as well, winking out of existence and leaving only empty air and a throbbing in my head and my hand.

I glance down at the ring, heavy and cold on my thumb. Wow.

A Winning Team

Whoa!" Wardell is at my side a second after the disk vanishes. Which is probably a good thing, since I stagger and almost topple over before he catches me. "Dude, that was intense! Did you do that?"

"Which part?" I mumble. It hurts to talk. It hurts to move. Heck, it hurts to think right now!

"The big, glowy thing in the middle of the room!" He looks at me like I'm a dummy, which right now I just might be. "The thing you taunted those two weird frozen freaks into jumping through." He scratches his head. "How'd you get them to jump through, exactly?"

"I didn't." I stagger over to the nearest bench and plop down onto it. Aaah. I might never move again. "They were charging me. I just made sure the disk was in their way." The ring is still digging into my thumb, so I slide it off and stick it back in my pocket. Then I start rubbing some warmth back into the thumb with my other hand. Much better.

"Seriously?" Now Wardell's looking at me like I'm nuts instead of lame. "I saw you standing there, and your mouth was moving, but I couldn't hear what you were saying over all the shouting and screaming and those icy creeps' grunting. You wanted them to make a play for you?"

"Yeah." I rub at my face with my unfrozen hand. "I couldn't think of anything else."

Wardell sits down next to me, causing the bench to creak a little. "Well, it worked," he admits. "Nice one." I just nod. "So — were those the ice zombies from that place you went?" I nod again. "Freaky."

Yeah, "freaky" about covers it.

Everybody's still in a panic, and there's lots of noise everywhere, creating a harsh buzzing in my head. But one particularly sharp voice is missing, and I look up, scanning the room. Why do I not hear her anywhere? I know she's — ah, there she is. Keisha is talking to Tariq, of course, off to one side. But she's doing it real quiet-like.

Uh-oh. Whenever she gets quiet, it's a really bad sign. Just like when she turns nice.

To make me worry even more, she and Tariq keep glancing over at me. That can't be good.

I wonder if she spotted the ring on my thumb. Everything was pretty crazy, and it isn't all that big, plus she wasn't near me, and there were ice zombies trying to bite her. Maybe she missed it.

And maybe I'll be named hall monitor, student of the year, class president, and soccer goalie all at the same time.

Right.

Some of the other kids are wandering over now, still a bit dazed but getting curious. "Hey, what was all that about?" One of them, Raymond, asks. "Those guys in makeup or something?"

"Yeah, and what was with that glowing circle?" Another, Terrence, adds. "Crazy special effects! They shooting a movie here and nobody told us?"

I don't really have any good answers — except the truth, which would sound totally insane and get me labeled the class nut — so I just shrug. "Yeah, I dunno," I tell them instead. "It was wacky, all right."

A few of the others join us, and people start offering

their own version of what that was all about. And, weirdly, I seem to be in the middle of the conversation. That never happens — most of the time it's just me and Wardell.

Which makes me realize he hasn't said anything since he declared the whole incident "freaky." It's been a few minutes at least, and not a peep.

That's not like him.

I turn, and almost fall off the bench.

Except for me, it's completely empty.

Where did Wardell go? For a second I worry that Zenon yanked him into the Zero Degree Zombie Zone, maybe to use as bait — you know, the whole, "Give me my ring or I torture your best friend!" trick. If that's the case, he's in for a big surprise. Nobody messes with my pal like that! I start to stand up, my knees a little shaky still —

— and that's when I see him.

Wardell.

And not with ice zombies.

No, this is even worse.

He's standing with Keisha and Tariq.

All three of them are talking, and gesturing, and smiling.

And laughing.

Laughing!

My worst enemies, my arch-nemeses, the banes of my existence, and my best friend is giggling with them like they're best buddies.

What the heck is going on here? Did I fall asleep and dream all this up? Did I slip into an alternate dimension? Did the ice zombies use some kind of reverse ray on all of us when nobody was looking?

Or is Wardell just suddenly hanging out with the enemy?

Keisha glances over, sees me, and smiles. It's not a

nice smile. It's her, "I'm gonna crush you like an insect" smile. I've seen it from her a lot today.

Then she turns back toward Wardell, and it's a totally different look on her face. Now it's her, "Hey, I'm perfectly nice and I like you and really want to hear what you have to say" look. The one she uses on teachers all the time. The same one she tried on me out in the hall earlier.

But this time it looks like it's working.

Because Wardell's smiling back at her. Not his, "Yeah, whatever, I'm watching you" smile, either. No, this is his, "Hey, yeah, totally cool" smile. Maybe even with traces of his, "I'm happy, everything's perfect, life is sweet" grin tossed in.

And Tariq, right next to him, is grinning, too. He slaps Wardell on the back, hard enough to make him stumble a little, but he's laughing when he does it. Like he wasn't trying to hurt Wardell at all, like this is all some big joke between friends.

Best friends.

The stab of pain that doubles me over this time isn't in my head. It's in my heart. And it hurts ten times worse than the one from the ring did.

Wardell. My best bud. My solo amigo. My pal, my home slice, my partner in crime.

Hanging with Tariq like they've been friends forever.

And not even looking my way.

No, wait, I'm wrong. He is looking my way. They all are.

And now they're heading over here.

The crowd around me thins, then fades to nothing as Keisha approaches, Tariq and Wardell right behind her. Tariq has one arm thrown over Wardell's broad shoulders like it's nothing, like they do this all the time. Wardell's nodding and bouncing to his own inner rhythm, like he does, and beaming like this is the day to end all days.

"Hey, Bakari," Keisha says, stopping a foot or two away from me. "How's it going?"

"Fine, thanks," I snap, though really my head's still pounding and my heart's still racing and my vision's a little blurry and my limbs feel like jelly. "How about you?"

"Oh, good, good," she says, waving off any concern. "Those guys were insane, right? What was the deal with them, exactly?" Same question I've heard from half our class at this point, only Keisha's staring at me like she knows I have a real answer.

I just shrug.

"Good job sending them back," she says next. She leans in a little closer. "But I think you got something that don't belong to you, don't you? And I'd like it back. Now."

I cross my arms, which is good because it stops them from shaking. "I don't know what you're talking about."

She snorts and rolls her eyes. Tariq laughs. He also elbows Wardell, like, "Hey, isn't that funny, yo?" Wardell chuckles, though he doesn't appear too happy about it. "Sure you do," Keisha corrects me. She's keeping her voice down, making sure this conversation stays private. "You got my ring. I want it back."

I look down at my hands. Good thing I stuffed it into my pocket again! "Nope, no ring here." I hold up both hands to prove it.

She sighs. "Fine, if that's how you want to play it. . . ." Then she shrugs. "Well, I guess that's a shame, then. I really liked that ring. But at least we've got something new to play with instead. Right, Tariq?"

Her cousin's been following along, and now he grins again. "Yeah, right." He reaches into his pocket, and I feel some of the headache come back guessing what he's going to pull out. Sure enough, when he opens his hand a second later he's got a round, pale-gray sphere nestled in his palm.

Granddad's marble.

"It sure is pretty," Keisha says to me, stepping back over to Tariq and admiring it. "Be a real shame if something happened to it. Especially if it means a lot to somebody." Her gaze flicks to Wardell and then back to me. Wardell gulps, looks at me, then looks away. Like he can't meet my eyes. Like he's done something horrible.

That traitor! I glare at him. I can't believe he told her about Granddad's marble! How could he betray me like that?

"What do you want, Keisha?" I ask. I'm impressed I manage to keep my own voice steady. No hint of the fear welling up inside, or the anger wrapped around it. Just steady, and cold, and hard.

"I want my ring back," she tells me, extending her open hand. "Give it to me, and you can have your grampa's precious stinky marble back. Deal?"

Yes, I want to shout. Yes! But once again I stop before my mouth opens. I want Granddad's marble back, sure. It means the world to me. And there's the whole, "Could be magic if Granddad wasn't just being weird" thing.

But this ring needs to go back to Zenon. Otherwise he's going to let loose with more ice zombies. Which only the ring can stop, so far. And I doubt Keisha's going to be willing to give it up if she gets it back.

My most precious keepsake from Granddad — or something that could save the whole world?

I shake my head. "No deal, Keisha."

"What?" She stares at me like she can't believe she heard right. "No deal? What're you talking about? It's my ring, fool! And your grampa's marble!" Now her scowl turns toward Wardell. "You said it was his most favorite possession!" she accuses.

Wardell looks at me instead of her. "Bakari, I —" he starts, but I cut him off.

"Don't even bother," I tell him, cold as I can manage. Cold as the ice zombies. "I got nothing to say to you." I stand up, wobbling for a second to catch my balance, then round on Keisha. "And as for you," I tell her, "you're not getting this ring back, and that's final!"

"Yeah?" she snaps back at me. "Well, we'll see, little loser boy. We'll see." Then she turns on her heel and stomps off. Tariq is right behind her, one arm still wrapped around Wardell's shoulder. Wardell takes one last look at me, something like shock on his round face, but I freeze him out and after a second he lets himself get led away.

Leaving me here, alone.

I fold my arms and put my head in them and just sit that way for a minute.

This is the worst day ever. What else can go wrong?

7

Enough Attitude to Go Around

Raargh!"

Why do I do this to myself? Every time I wonder if things could get worse — they do. And yet I keep asking it, over and over again. When will I ever learn?

Sigh.

I lift my head and look around. Oh good, more ice zombies.

There are four of them this time. One looks a lot like one of the zombies from before, the one that swiped at me. Maybe it is him, and he found a way back. It's hard to tell when they're so tall, and so frozen, and all zombie-fied.

The second one is a little shorter than the first, but twice as wide. Really, he's like two of the first guy standing together. His legs are really thick, too — they'd have

to be, to be strong enough to lug that big body around —
but his arms are normal, so they look super skinny on
him. And maybe a little short. Weird. He's like the ice
zombie version of a T. rex, I guess.

The third one's a woman. Even with all the ice
and zombie-ism, you can tell. Not that she's pretty or
anything — she's an ice zombie, ew! — but she's definitely not built like a guy.

The last one's shorter than the others, almost Tariq's
height, and kind of built like him, too. Muscular but not
hulking, more slim and solid. He doesn't have his arms
up like the others, either. They're down at his sides like
a normal person. He walks normally, too, no lumbering.
If it wasn't for the fact that his skin is pale blue and his
hair's all icy and his eyes are all filmy, you'd think he
was a normal kid or a small adult. He hangs back behind
the others, letting them stumble into the room doing the
whole growling-and-arm-waving routine, and just watches
for a bit.

I don't like it.

Not that I like his three friends, either, but at least
them I can understand.

When did my life get so strange that ice zombies

terrorizing my class during lunch was something I could understand and treat like it was normal?

Everybody's running around screaming again, of course. Why wouldn't they be? There's a quartet of ice zombies surrounding us! Lots of snarling, lots of grunting, lots of tables and trays and books being tossed around and banged about.

It's a wonder none of the teachers or lunch staff have come in to get a better look at what's going on around here.

Then again, maybe somebody peeked in, saw ice zombies, and decided they'd just sit this one out.

I wish I could do the same.

Instead I haul myself to my feet, reach into my pocket, and pull out the ring. "Here we go again," I mutter as I slip the clunky ice jewelry over my thumb and hold it up.

Nothing happens.

"Let's go!" I shout, shaking it like I did last time. "Make with the cold and the disk and all that! Now!" I glare at the ring, squeezing it tight again, and concentrate.

Nothing happens.

Keisha is suddenly there next to me, her hand out. "Give it to me!"

"What? No way!" I twist away from her, hold it higher — she's one of the only people in our class who's about my height, and Tariq is still on the other side of the room, using a lunch tray to batter the ice zombie woman away from Trisha and some others — and I try again.

Still nothing.

"Work, darn it!" I shake it more, squeeze it tighter, practically cross my eyes trying to mentally activate it.

Nothing.

Not even a little blue blip.

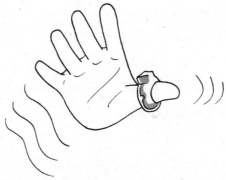

"Bakari!" It's Keisha again. "Give it to me! Now!"

And there's her hand, right there.

You know what? Fine. I tug the ring off and slap it into her palm. "You want it," I tell her, "fine. Here. Take it. Now make them go away!"

She slides the ring onto her own thumb, studies it

there, and smiles her smug little cat-with-the-cream smile. "With pleasure."

I watch as she raises her hand, ring out like some kind of weapon. "Ring, ring, do your thing!" she shouts.

And a dazzling blue disk appears in the middle of the room, hovering high above, looking like a big, floating halo. Just like that.

"Okay, you got it to work," I admit. "But it's not like they're all the way up there, are they?"

She grins at me, then flicks her hand at the disk — and it glides across the room like it was a Frisbee and she just gave it a proper toss. It sails straight for the biggest zombie, the super-wide one —

— and drops right over his head. Clearly Keisha is the queen of ringtoss.

The zombie has just enough time to look a little surprised before his head disappears. The disk keeps dropping, swallowing the rest of him, and when it hits the floor he's gone, gone, gone.

Why didn't I think of that? It's a whole lot easier than maneuvering two ice zombies to jump through the hoop from opposite sides!

"Tariq!" Keisha calls next. He bats the ice zombie

woman away and looks over. "Catch!" With another flick she somehow sends the disk skipping across the floor toward him. If this was a lake and it was a stone she'd win, easy.

Tariq catches it with one hand, grins, waves it like a salute, and then turns and lassos the ice zombie woman with it. I'm not quite sure why his fingers don't disappear, too — maybe because they're connected to the rest of him, and there's a lot more of him outside the disk than in — but anyway he slides the disk down over her and sends her back where she belongs.

Which leaves two, the regular-sized one and the smaller, more normal-acting one.

He goes for the regular ice zombie — How does a phrase like that even make sense? What's "regular" about an ice zombie? — stalking it like it's a tiger and he's a big-game hunter, the disk held out in front him like a combination shield and spear. The ice zombie sees Tariq coming but it's clearly not too bright, and decides to meet him head on.

One quick swipe of the disk and we're down to just one.

This one watches Tariq approach, head tilted to one side, studying him. It waits until he's close — and then it darts forward, fast, and shoves him hard.

Tariq goes flying. The disk comes loose and rolls across the floor. Tariq slams into one of the lunch tables. Ouch.

And the ice zombie shifts its focus to Keisha.

Who I'm standing right next to.

Not that Keisha seems worried. "Oh, you want some of this?" she tells him as he stalks toward her. This one actually moves like it's a tiger, careful and graceful and slow for now but with that coiled speed you can see in every stride. Keisha just glares. "Well, come get some, then!"

Suddenly he bursts into a sprint, but Keisha's ready for him, and the blue disk appears right in his path. Somehow he manages to twist to the side, dodging the opening — but then it swivels right in his way again. He turns, and it follows. The disk glides forward, and he backs up a pace, then bolts forward, sliding around it before Keisha can change its course.

It's like watching a weird dance, the disk trying to close the distance, the zombie trying to increase it.

Right now, it looks to me like the zombie's winning.

Which doesn't sit too well with Keisha. "Oh, I'm done with this," she mutters, and I see her scowl. She raises her hand again — and a second disk appears right behind the zombie. Then a third, on his left. And finally a fourth, on his right.

He's boxed in.

Just before the disks converge, blocking him completely from sight, I see the ice zombie look over at Keisha and nod. He's paying her respect.

That's one clever ice zombie.

Then the disks move in, linking together to become one big wraparound shape — and squeeze into a single sphere before flattening again and winking out.

No more ice zombies.

"Nice one," I tell Keisha. I don't really want to, but it's true. She's way better at using the ring than I am.

She just sniffs. "It's all about control," she tells me, like it's no big deal she just fought off four ice zombies with nothing but a magic ring. "I have that in spades, and this here ring knows it." The way she scans me and dismisses me says without words that she thinks I don't have it. I guess she's right. Making the ring produce one disk almost wiped me out. She did four at once. But she's always had a lot of confidence. Me? Not so much.

Tariq comes ambling over, all casual now that the ice zombies are gone. Behind him, some kids are starting to push the lunch tables back into place. "Good looking out, cos," he tells Keisha, and bumps fists with her.

Wardell is right behind him, like some oversized shadow. "Yeah, that was awesome," he agrees, offering a fist, but both cousins ignore him. "So, what do you two wanna do next?"

The look Keisha turns his way could fry an egg, and if I weren't still mad at Wardell I'd feel sorry for him. "Back off, kid," she tells him in almost a snarl. "We're done with you."

"Done? What do you mean? I thought we were friends." He turns toward Tariq. "Tariq? Aren't we friends?"

Tariq shrugs and studies his shoes. If I didn't know better, I'd think he actually felt bad for Wardell, too. Not Keisha, though. She just barks out a sharp little laugh. "Friends? Oh, heck no!" She laughs again and looks my way. "We just needed you to get my ring back from this no-name, no-neck loser." She sniffs. "You couldn't even do that right! But at least you let slip about the marble being his. That was almost useful."

Let slip? So Wardell didn't betray me on purpose? I should have known. He's always had my back, all these years. Why would I think he'd turn on me now?

"Wardell —" I start, but he puts up a hand.

"I'm done with you, Bakari, I'm not speaking to you anymore," he tells me. I don't bother to point out how that was speaking to me. I don't think he'd appreciate it much right at this moment.

So instead I turn to Keisha. "You can't keep that ring,"

I tell her. "The guy sending these ice zombies? It's his ring. We need to get it back to him before he lets all of them loose and they take over the world." Though I'm not entirely sure what they'd do with the world once they had it. Freeze it? Eat everyone? Freeze and eat everyone? Freeze everyone and just eat a few of us? I don't know that Zenon's really thought this whole thing through.

Not that Keisha seems to care. "Whatever," she says, waving off what I just said. "You're just sore 'cause you can't work its magic."

Anything I wanted to say in response gets interrupted as Mrs. Crump steps into the cafeteria. "All done with lunch?" she asks, glancing around. I look, too. Amazingly, all the furniture's back in place, all the trash is cleaned up, and we're all standing near the door. If you didn't know better, and didn't notice the dents and scrapes everywhere, you'd never think anything unusual had happened here. "Library time," Mrs. Crump continues. "Form your lines, please!"

Keisha struts off without a second glance, right up to the door and Mrs. Crump, that ice ring still settled around her thumb. I mutter and grumble under my breath as I follow the other boys to stand over behind Tariq.

I just know this isn't gonna end well.

8

Never Trust a Zombie Lord

This is lousy! Wardell won't look at me, much less talk to me. Can't say I blame him. How could I think he'd hurt me? What is wrong with me that I can't even trust my best friend?

I'm trudging along, staring at my own dirty-sneakered feet, not paying a whole lot of attention, when we round the last corner to the library.

Brzzzzzz!

That's when I get hit with a blast of cold air strong enough to make my breath instantly turn to those little puffs, like cloud rings.

Great. Just great.

Glancing up, I see another disk has appeared, not two feet in front of me. No arms grabbing for me this time, at least, but the circle itself is producing some kind of pull like a giant vacuum cleaner.

Oh no!

I'm being sucked in!

And I'm not the only one. During our walk from the cafeteria the lines shifted order again, like when Keisha and Tariq cornered me and Wardell on the way to lunch. This time, I guess I was walking faster than I realized, and everybody else just got out of my way. However it happened, I'm now second in line for the boys. Which means I'm right behind Tariq.

And as the disk starts tugging harder from the side, and I feel my feet slipping across the floor, I see that he's being pulled toward that frozen opening, too.

"Get back!" I shout at him, trying to wave him off. I see him plant his feet and hunch over, like he can stick himself to the floor through sheer force of will, but it's no good. The disk's too strong, and we're both sliding toward it.

"Bakari!" It's Wardell, shoving his way through the crowd. "What's happening?"

"It's Zenon!" I tell him. "He's pulling me back in!" I'm almost to the disk now. There's nothing to grab on

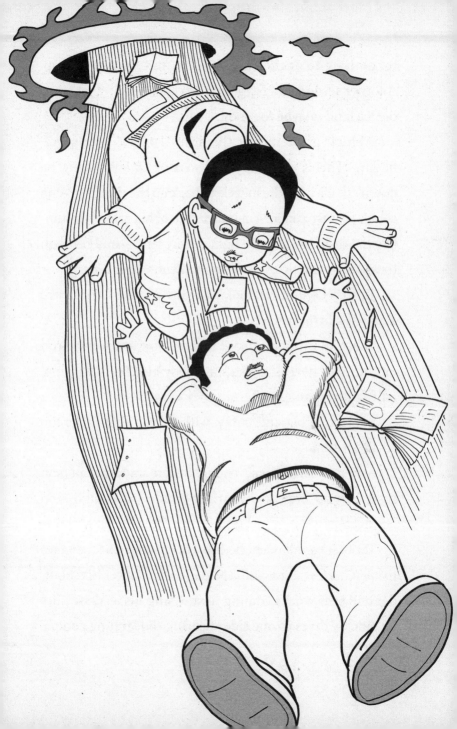

to, nothing to anchor myself with, and no way to stop. Another second and I'm gonna be right back in that zombie ice land, maybe for good.

Wardell grabs me by the arm. "I'm not letting go!" he says. This is why Wardell is so cool. Unfortunately, he doesn't really have the muscle to back up the thought. Who could, against Zenon? I'm pulled free of his grip and stumble, the disk yanking me right off my feet — and through that plane of arctic cold, right into Zenon's homeland.

Tariq is behind me, looking really annoyed, confused, and just a little scared.

What I didn't expect, as I hit the snow and ice and roll out of his way, was to see somebody else half-charging, half-falling through after him.

Somebody big and bulky, with a head that looks too small for him.

And as if that wasn't enough, there's another person right behind him, with a mass of hair piled high atop her head.

Tariq staggers when he hits the ground but manages to keep his feet. Show-off. He glances back over his shoulder and sees what's coming next. Using his athletic gifts he quickly dives to one side, clearing the landing zone.

Bam!

Wardell hits with a thunderclap.

Keisha's right behind him and plows into him, bouncing off Wardell's midsection and back into a nearby snowbank.

The disk vanishes.

There's nothing but ice and snow all around.

My best friend and my two worst enemies are in the thick of this icy horror. And, somewhere, not too far off, are a whole lot of ice zombies.

It's like a crazy snow day.

Tariq's the first one to say anything. "Where are we?" he asks, rubbing his arms and trying not to shiver. "This

place is freezing! And what's the deal with all those glowing circles, anyway?" Keisha stumbles out of the snowbank, sputtering angrily and brushing snow from her clothes, and he turns to her. "Did you make it do that? You made the ones in the lunchroom, right?"

"No, I didn't make it do that," she snaps at him, shaking her head and sending snow flying from her hair. "The ones at lunch — yeah, those were mine, but only because I saw Bakari do it first, so I knew that was how to get rid of those freaks." She glares at me. "Did you bring us here, wherever here is? Where are we, in some kind of ice rink or something?"

I can't help it — I laugh. "Does this look like an ice rink to you?" I ask, gesturing all around us. There are houses off a ways on one side and trees on the other.

However, here in the middle we're in what looks like a park or a parking lot — wide and flat and open. "This is the Zero Degree Zombie Zone. It's where those ice zombies at lunch came from. And it's where the zombie ruler I told you about lives — he's the one who wants the ring."

"Yeah?" Keisha frowns and scans the area. She rubs the ring with the fingers of her other hand. "Well, he can't have it."

"I don't know," Tariq offers. "Maybe we should give it to him. Maybe then he'll send us home."

Whoa! That may be the first time I've ever heard Tariq disagree with Keisha. I stare at him, but no more than she does. Before she can say anything, though, I find myself talking — and saying something I never thought I'd say, not in a zillion years.

"Actually, Keisha may be right." It sounds like my voice, and I can feel my mouth moving, but I'm surprised by what I'm saying. As surprised as the others are, judging by their expressions. "I know I said before that we should return the ring to Zenon, but now that he's dragged us here I'm not sure that's a good idea. If we do give it up, we've got no leverage, nothing to bargain with."

Wardell nods. "Yeah, he'll hold all the cards. That can't be good for us."

I'm looking around, and I see a bunch of tall figures heading our way from the direction of the houses. "Hide it, quick," I warn Keisha. "And don't anybody let on we have it."

For once she doesn't say anything back. She just nods and slips the ring off her thumb and into a pocket somewhere. I don't see where, which is probably for the best. Anyway, I'm too busy watching the ice zombies approach.

There are five of them, plus Zenon himself. He's taller than any of them by at least four heads, and his walk's not as stiff. Plus, there are the eyes — his sharp blue ones versus their blank white ones. No mistaking who's in charge here. Especially since he calls out to me as soon as he's close enough.

"Welcome back, Bakari Katari Johnson!" Still using my whole name — maybe ice zombies, even ice zombie lords, don't understand how names work on Earth? Maybe Zenon is his whole name, and everyone here just has the one name, so he figures my full name is the name I need to be called each and every time? Or maybe he just knows it annoys me. Anyway, he's still talking so I force myself to pay attention again. "And this time you have brought your friends!" Well, *friend*, I correct in my head, but I'm not gonna tell him that. Though it might be better for Tariq and Keisha if I did.

"We are no friends of his," Keisha snaps. That figures. "Bakari Bad Breath? Not a chance. We were just standing too close when you sent that circle to collect him, and got

pulled in with the fool." She straightens to her full height and scowls up at Zenon, who's now closed the distance to us and looks like a skyscraper beside her. "So just whip up another of those disks and we'll be on our way."

"I don't think so." The smile he gives her is all teeth, like a jungle cat about to pounce. "My zombies are hungry, after all. I didn't let those I sent through before eat anyone, because I wanted to make sure Bakari Katari Johnson would not be obstructed in his return. But now that you are here, I see no reason not to feed you to them. They deserve a reward for such patience."

"Look Zenon, we crushed your dumb zombies like icicles. Nobody's feeding anybody to anyone," I tell him, standing my ground when he turns those ice-laser eyes and that sparkling shark smile on me. "Not if you want your ring back."

In an instant he's covered the space between us and is leaning in over me. "You have it? Where is it?"

"I don't have it," I tell him. "Not on me, anyway." Which is at least partially true. "And I'm not gonna tell you where it is, either. You let us go back — all of us — and I'll get it for you, but not before."

"Hm." Zenon strokes his chin, staring down at me. Finally he chuckles. "Well done, Bakari Katari Johnson," he says slowly. "Well done. I had planned to simply take the ring and then feed you to my zombies, but now things are going to get even more interesting. Are you lying to me? Do you have it on you? If so, I can stay with my original plan — I get my ring back, my zombies get a good meal, and I regain total access to your world. But can I risk it? If you are telling the truth, killing you now would cost me the ring, and I need it if I plan to open enough portals for a proper invasion. Hm." He goes back to stroking his chin. "Yes, clever indeed."

Keisha lets out a little snort, like she can't believe anyone's calling me clever. Bad idea on her part, because it draws Zenon's attention. "You say you don't have the ring," he muses, studying her with those icy blue eyes, "but that doesn't mean it isn't here, does it? Perhaps one of you has it. Do *you*, my dear?" He looms over Keisha again.

Fortunately, she's not easily intimidated. Not Keisha. "You think I'd take anything that fool offered me?" she asks, squinting her eyes. "Please! Anything he touches is gonna have loser stink all over it, and I don't want any part of that!"

Zenon's eyes go wider — I guess he's not used to anyone speaking to him like that, without any fear — and he scowls a little, but he doesn't pursue it any further. Whew! Instead his gaze swivels back toward me. "I will give you a few moments, Bakari Katari Johnson," he announces. "To ponder your fate. Know that toying with me is ill-advised, for I have little patience and a great many hungry followers." He turns and stomps away, taking his little ice zombie posse with him.

"Whew! Man, that was close!" Wardell blurts out as soon as they've gone. "I thought they'd figure it out for sure!"

Keisha smiles. "Nah, I had it covered." She looks at me, and it's not a look I'm used to from her. It's not smug or snarky or nasty. More . . . considering. "You was telling the truth about him, before," she says after a minute, and her voice is quieter than usual, and without any spikiness. "And about the ring."

I nod.

"We've gotta get it out of here, away from him," she declares. "And ourselves back to Thurgood Cleavon Wilson Elementary."

Another nod.

Then she sighs. "Any idea how?"

"Try the ring," I suggest. "You opened disks to here before, maybe you can open one away from here now."

She nods, retrieves the ring, slides it back onto her thumb, and waves it in the air. "Ring, ring, do your thing," she orders, shaking it about. "Get us back to school, double-time!" Nothing happens.

She tries again before lowering her hand. "I'm not feeling it," she confesses. "Before, it was like this jab of cold in my brain, like the worst brain freeze ever. Now, nothing."

Huh. I'm not sure why that is, but Wardell offers an idea. "Maybe it's 'cause we're here and not home," he says. "Maybe on our side you can use it to open disks to here because you're from home and it's from here, but now you're here so it's not working."

That actually makes some sense. "And Zenon could use it to make disks into our world because he's from here," I say. "The ring's a key but it only works from whatever side of the door you're from."

Wardell nods and grins at me. This is just like when he and I hang out after school, coming up with all sorts of crazy ideas and bouncing them around all afternoon. Only, of course, this time it's real and we're liable to get eaten by ice zombies, which takes away some of the fun.

"So that ring's useless here?" Tariq asks. His skin's looking a little blue and he's shivering. So are the rest of us. "How're we gonna get home, then?"

Looking at him, I have an idea. "My marble," I say. "Give it to me."

Keisha snorts. "We're freezing and about to be zombie food and all you can think about is your dumb marble? Really?"

"That dumb marble may be the only thing that can save our butts," I snap back. I hold out my hand. "Give it up, Tariq."

He glances over at Keisha, then at me, then back at her, then back at me. Finally he shrugs and pulls it from his jacket pocket, dropping it into my palm. "Yeah, sure."

The second the marble touches my skin, I feel whole again.

And maybe something else, too. "Come on, Granddad," I mutter, closing my fist around it tight. "You always said it was magic, and right now that's exactly what I need. Light, courage, power, right? Well, I got the courage. Give me the power!"

There's no glowing disk, but I do feel warm all of a sudden, like there's heat radiating out from my hand. And the air all around me starts to shimmer. "Grab hold of me, quick!" I tell the others. Wardell latches onto my shoulder at once, and Tariq grabs my other one, with Keisha wrapping both hands around his arm. Good thing, too, because the shimmering is growing, the whole ice world is blurring around us, all of it fading in a big ball of light and warmth and color —

— and then everything snaps back into focus and we're in the hall in front of the library again, like nothing happened. Except for the puddle at our feet.

"There you are!" Mrs. Crump says, appearing around the corner of the library. "I was wondering where you four had gone! Come on, come on, the rest of the class is inside already!" she says, ushering us into the library. We all follow her without a word. I wish I thought that was the end of it, but I know it isn't.

9

Truths, Plans, and Consequences

What the heck are we gonna do about all this?" Keisha corners me the second we're in the library. Mrs. Crump has ditched us again — she's off talking to the librarian, Ms. Braithwaite. It doesn't matter, we all know the drill. Pick up a book and sit and read quietly the whole period, then check it out at the end if we want. So basically this is a free period — if you know how to sit with a book open and keep your voice down, you can just hang out and talk the whole time.

Before I can grab a book, Keisha shoves me toward a corner table. She slaps a book into my hands from one of the bookshelves as we pass and grabs another for herself. Tariq scoops up a paperback, and Wardell simply pulls a comic from his backpack as we all drop into chairs. We're

far enough away from everybody else that they won't hear what we're saying. Okay, I'm sure it might look strange seeing the four of us sitting together, especially with Tariq battling me for hall monitor.

Then again, our quartet is hardly the most interesting event of the day. First off, there was all that weirdness in the cafeteria. Even if they didn't figure out that we were dealing with ice zombies, they at least saw two freaky-looking guys come in and start terrorizing everybody. Someone had to see me make them disappear through a glowing blue disk. I'm sure nosy Niecy Washington saw four more zombies show up, trashing the lunchroom and trying to bite people. She probably also hung around to see that it was Keisha who made more glowing disks appear and swallow the zombies up.

But did anyone notice that another blue disk appeared on the way to the library, and that this one swallowed *us* up — me and Keisha and Tariq and Wardell? Some of the others must've seen that, especially since most of them hadn't even reached the library when it happened. Yet nobody's saying anything, or even glancing our way. And Mrs. Crump wondered where we'd gone but didn't freak out about our disappearing into a blue circle of ice? So she didn't see anything and nobody said anything to her. At this moment I can't decide if I'm grateful to my classmates for keeping our secret or mad at them for not caring enough to alert our teacher when we vanished into another dimension.

"Why we gotta do anything?" Tariq asks, flipping his book open to a random page. I didn't see the cover clearly enough to read the title, but it had a big bullet train on the front. Mine's about some kid detective, I think. It's not like I'm really paying much attention to it at the moment. "We're outta there, right?" Tariq continues. "And you still got that ring, safe and sound. It's all good, right?"

Wardell sets down his comic and rolls his eyes. "Did this Zenon zombie lord guy need that ring to make that big hole we all fell through?" he asks, completely ignoring the fact that he's talking to the most popular fourth grader at Thurgood Cleavon Wilson Elementary. I've gotta admit, I'm glad to see him dressing Tariq down like this, standing up for himself. "No. Clearly he can reach through to our world without the ring. It just lets him do it more, bigger, faster."

"Right, he said something about needing it to open

enough portals for a proper invasion," I remember out loud. "He can definitely still come after us without it. And he will. He wants that ring bad."

"What if we give it to him?" Keisha asks. "You got that marble, and it got us back home. Maybe it can shut down circles fast as he can open them."

"I don't know," I tell her. "Maybe. Is that a chance we want to take, though? What if it can't keep him out, him and all those ice zombies of his? What if it can only close half of them, or a third, or all but one or two, even? If even a few of those things get loose . . ." I trail off, not wanting to finish that sentence. I don't have to.

We all go quiet for a minute, thinking. I use that time to tap Wardell on the shoulder. "I'm sorry, Wardell," I say. "I should've trusted you. You've always had my back. I just, when you were over there talking to them, and then you three came over together, and she knew about Granddad's marble —"

Wardell smiles like when he sees string cheese. "I get it. I didn't mean to say anything, it just slipped out how important it was to you." He glances at Keisha and Tariq. "And I gotta admit, I knew they didn't really like me, but it still felt good when they acted like they did."

Tariq studies his book like it's going to be on the next test. "Sorry about that," he mutters after a second. He looks up and meets Wardell's gaze. "That wasn't cool, jerking you around like that." I don't know that I've ever heard him apologize before. This is a day of firsts.

I almost fall out of my chair, though, when Keisha says, "Yeah, I'm sorry, too." At first I think she means for mistreating Wardell, but she's looking at me. "I kind of got you into this whole mess," she admits. "I found the ring this morning, out in the hall. I'd got in early and saw your name on the sign-up sheet. I was ducking back out to text Tariq a heads-up when I saw the ring, just laying there on the floor." She frowns and looks away. "When I picked it up, I was still going off about you and how you were gonna regret ever signing up."

I jump up, then sit down quickly when Mrs. Crump glances over. "That's why Zenon said he heard my name! The first time he grabbed me, it was out in the hall between class and the bathroom! That was probably the same spot where he dropped the ring in the first place. And somehow he heard you when you picked it up, and heard you say my name!"

She nods. "Yeah, that's the way I figured it, too."

We all just sit there for a minute. But finally I clear my throat.

"Okay, so we're all sorry," I say. "That's super. Now we've just got to figure out a way to stop Zenon from getting his hands on this ring and invading the world, while not getting eaten by ice zombies ourselves." Piece of apple pie. Sure.

Keisha pulls out the ring and taps it with a fingernail. "It's like a key, right?" she says slowly. "It lets us open those holes to his world, or him open them to here." I nod but don't say anything, because I can see she's got more. "And your marble, that was like a key, too, at least that time."

"Yeah," I say. "Not sure that's what it usually does, but it did the trick when we needed it."

She locks eyes with me. "What if we use them together? You with your marble, me with this ring? And what if we try doing the same thing at the same time? And that thing is locking the door for good — all the doors, in fact — so he can't come through here ever?"

I think that over. "It might work," I agree. "Like turning the key in the lock and snapping it off so the lock's jammed." I smile. "Let's give it a try."

"Rock on!" Wardell says, grinning. "Grab those magic stones, roll some bones, it's time to save the world!"

Tariq rolls his eyes and Keisha glares at Wardell, but I grin right back at him and we bump fists. Whether this works or not, I'm glad I've got my best friend back.

10

Locking It Down

We can't do this in here, can we?" I ask, scanning the library. Mrs. Crump is done gabbing with Ms. Braithwaite and is now sitting in an armchair near the librarian's desk, flipping through a magazine. The rest of our class is milling about like usual, pretending to read, but I'm pretty sure everybody'd notice if we pulled out an ice ring and a magic marble and started doing stuff with them.

Keisha clearly thinks the same thing, since she gives me her patented, "Were you absent the day they handed out brains?" look. "We need someplace private, duh," she tells me.

Something else occurs to me, too. "We should be near that first disk," I say as the four of us rise to our feet. "It's right where you found the ring in the first place, so it's like the first door."

She nods. "Yeah, and nobody'll be around there right now. Nice."

Wardell gulps. "Only question is, how're we gonna get out there when we're supposed to be in here?" he asks.

Tariq smiles. "Leave that to me," he says as he leads us over to Mrs. Crump.

"Is there a problem?" our teacher asks, glancing up from her magazine as we approach. It's about gardening, I notice. Does Mrs. Crump even garden?

Tariq shrugs and hits her with his golden-boy smile, full wattage. "Bakari and Wardell left some stuff behind in the cafeteria," he explains. "Lunch was . . . a little crazy today." You can say that again, I think. "Is it okay if Keisha and I accompany them back there to get their things? We won't take long — we'll be back before library is over."

It all sounds so smart, and of course he and Keisha can do no wrong in the eyes of any adult, so I'm not all that surprised when Mrs. Crump says, "That sounds fine, Tariq. Thank you for offering." Her gaze switches to me and Wardell. "Try to be a little more careful where you leave your things next time, you two. Now run along and hurry

back." Then she goes back to her magazine. Who knew flowers could be so fascinating?

"Smooth," I tell Tariq as we head out of the library. He just shrugs, but he looks pleased. Must be nice to use his evil powers for good for a change.

"Don't we need a hall pass or something, though?" Wardell asks.

Keisha smirks at him. "Why would you? You've got the class's hall monitor with you instead." She's eyeing me when she says that last bit. Yeah, Keisha, I got it, thanks.

The four of us trek down the hall, stopping right about where I remember being grabbed. "Yeah," Keisha agrees, "I found the ring right over there." She points at a spot between us and the nearest wall. "This is definitely the place." She raises her hand — I hadn't noticed she was wearing the ice ring again already — and I quickly pull out Granddad's marble. "You ready?"

"Uh, sure." At least, I think so. But ready or not, looks like we're doing this, so I don't have much choice.

"Okay, on three," Keisha orders. For once I don't mind letting her tell me what to do. I just close my eyes, squeeze the marble tight, and concentrate. "One," she calls out. "Two. Three!"

I hear her muttering, "Ring, ring, do your thing" like she did last time, but I'm busy with my own words. "Light, courage, power," I remind the marble, thinking of Granddad and his wisdom, his comfort, but also his faith in this marble — and mine, too, especially after it brought us back here from Zenon's frozen zombie zone.

"Come on, marble, help me out here," I whisper to it. "Lend me some of that power so we can make this place zombie-proof for good."

I feel the marble warming in my hand, and there's a wash of something over me. It feels like . . . happiness. Peace. Protection. "I've got it going!" I say out loud.

"So do I!" Keisha replies, and I blink. I hadn't even realized I had my eyes shut. She's right beside me, ring held high — and there's a blue disk forming in front of us.

"We're trying to close them all down," I remind her quickly, "not open new ones!"

"I'm not doing that!" she shouts back. I don't know why we're shouting, except there's a whooshing sound coming from the disk, like a fierce wind is blowing through it. Actually, there is a wind, and it's bitterly cold — I can feel it biting through my T-shirt and jeans. Man! I don't remember the disks doing this before! Then again, most of the time I was either being yanked through them or concentrating on not getting munched on, so I was probably a little distracted. Still, this can't be good.

"You're not? Then who —" I don't bother to finish that question. There's no need. Not when a tall, pale-blue figure steps through the disk and turns toward us, growling as it reaches down with long, pale, frozen arms. Ice zombie!

"Crap! Zenon must know what we're up to!" Keisha yells. "He's gonna try stopping us!" She shoves the ice zombie away with her free hand. "Well, nobody shuts Keisha Marie Owens down, you hear?"

I like her tone for a change, and I agree that we've got to stand firm. That's going to be tough to do, though, as a second ice zombie follows the first into our world. This hall's starting to get mighty crowded.

Then a familiar athletic figure leaps forward and tackles the first ice zombie around the knees, knocking him to the ground. "Go ahead and do what you gotta do," Tariq tells us over his shoulder, leaping to his feet and charging the second zombie. "I got this."

"*We* got this," a second voice corrects, and I almost drop the marble in surprise when I see Wardell barrel into the other ice zombie from behind. He uses his own bulk to stagger the frozen fiend, making the arctic ghoul go right into Tariq's tackle. Nice one, Wardell!

But that first one's getting back to his feet — slowly, sure, like some aging grandpa, but getting there nonetheless. And he's behind Tariq and Wardell now. I take a step forward. I've got to help them!

A hand on my shoulder brings me back around. "We've got to keep going," Keisha tells me, and she's not mocking, not snubbing, not even sneering or playing. She's serious as she adds, "This may be the only chance we've got."

I nod. She's right. "Behind you!" I shout, letting Tariq and Wardell know to watch their backs. They both turn, and soon Wardell's swinging his backpack like a hammer, beating the one zombie back while Tariq handles the other. I try to drown out the sound of them whaling on those ice zombies and focus on my marble again. The warm feeling never left, and now it's ramping up further. I feel like my whole body should be glowing from it, but I've got my eyes shut again so I can't tell for sure.

I do hear more grunts and growls, and at one point something cold brushes past my arm like a snowman just pushed by me. Judging from all the noise, there's a lot more than just two ice zombies here with us now. Zenon's definitely onto us, and he's pulling out all the stops, sending through as many of his frozen army as he can, trying to cut us off before we can finish.

But I also hear shouts and grunts that are definitely plain old human, and that means Tariq and Wardell are holding their own. For now. I don't know how much longer that's gonna last, though, so I tune out the sounds of my best friend and my worst enemy fighting for all our lives and throw everything I have into what I'm doing instead. If Keisha and I can't pull this off, they're fighting in vain. This has got to work!

I feel the moment when it does, too. There's almost a click in my head, and the warmth shifts, somehow. It's still there, still wrapped around me like a cozy blanket, but now it's extending outward, enveloping something else as well. Something right nearby, bigger than I am, and really cold. The door! The marble's magic has got the door in its grip, the first door, the one that symbolizes every passage between this world and Zenon's! I feel the cold wind stop, the air settling, and there's no new monster sounds emerging beside me. We're doing it!

"I've got it shut tight!" I tell Keisha, my eyes still closed. I can feel that I'm right, though. I'm holding the door shut for her. "Time to break the key off in the lock!"

"On it!" she replies, a strain in her voice I haven't heard before. I know she's putting everything into this, too. And one thing you've gotta say about Keisha Marie Owens, the girl doesn't like to lose. I know she's not going to quit until we get this done.

Again there's a feeling, this one a little different. I can already sense the marble holding the door shut. Now I feel the extra pressure that's coming from Keisha and that ring — the ring that was made to open the door and is now being used to close it. And lock it. For good.

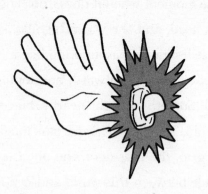

There's a loud click — more like a snap, really — and something in the air changes again. The wind had already vanished, and most of the cold, but now it's actually getting warm around us instead, a general heat I can feel right through the ring's protection.

And then I hear moaning. Ice zombie moaning. Not the scary, "I'm gonna eat your face" kind, though. No, this moaning sounds . . . scared.

I open my eyes again and blink. The disk is still there, but it's visibly shrinking. "We did it!" I shout, turning and grabbing Keisha in a hug before I even realize what I'm doing. "We did it!"

She hugs me back, just for a second before she gently pushes me away. "Yeah," she agrees, grinning as big as I've ever seen her. "We sure did, didn't we?"

Then there's a rushing sound. It's coming from the disk, which is pulling the ice zombies back toward it.

Unfortunately, we're between them and the disk, and it starts tugging on us, too.

Uh-oh.

11

Doors Work Both Ways

Get out of the way!" I shout, moving Keisha to one side and diving to the other. Just in time, too. One of the ice zombies goes sliding past, scrabbling on the floor with its long, sharp, frozen fingers as it's dragged kicking and screaming — flailing and moaning — back through the disk. Another one almost hooks my ankle with one hand but I kick him in the arm instead, and as he yanks back his arm he sails past me. Two down, however many to go.

This won't be easy. I still feel something tugging me. Either the disk isn't too picky, the ring and the marble make us fair game, or we're just too close for it to care.

"Hold on to something!" Keisha yells, grabbing a locker handle with both hands and clinging on for dear life. I do the same on the other side. Another ice zombie careens past us, shooting between us and into the disk, which is now about my height but hanging a few feet off the ground.

The wind's still whistling into it — in this time, not out — and a quick peek around shows more ice zombies starting to slide its way. Just how many did Zenon send through, anyway? And how did Tariq and Wardell manage to hold all of them off for so long?

For that matter, where are Tariq and Wardell? I don't see either of them. With my grip on the locker handle barely secure, I don't dare twist around too much. Another ice zombie zooms by, wailing, and disappears through the disk. Then another. Is it me, or are they picking up speed?

Then I hear a squeak just below me. I glance down. My sneakers are starting to slide, slowly, across the floor.

Toward that disk!

I try dragging them back, but it's no good. The pull is stronger than I am.

Soon my body's stretched out, hands still clutching the locker, feet straining toward the opening.

Another second and both feet leave the ground completely. Now I'm sideways, and holding on desperately.

And my fingers, all sweaty from fear and excitement

and probably dripping from melted ice as well, are starting to lose their grip.

"I'm slipping!" I call out.

"Me, too!" Keisha replies, and I glance over. Sure enough, she's about as bad off as I am. We're both hanging like flags in a stiff wind. The disk is down to the size of a Hula-Hoop now, but that's still plenty big enough to swallow both of us whole.

And with the key broken off, if we sail through that disk now, we'll be trapped in Zenon's Zero Degree Zombie Zone forever.

Though I have a feeling Zenon wouldn't exactly let us alone for that long.

I shift my grip, almost getting pulled loose in the process, but I manage to get a slightly better hold as a result. Whew!

And then the last zombie zooms by and rams into me with its hard, icy shoulder.

"NO!" My shout emerges at the exact second my fingers are torn away from the locker by the impact, but there's nothing I can do. I scrape my fingers across the locker door as I go sliding past it, but there's nothing else to grab onto, and I'm already too far away to try again.

Across the hall I hear an echoing scream, and look up from my own predicament to see that Keisha's come loose, too. I don't know if the ice zombie bumped her as well or if she just couldn't hold on, but it doesn't really matter.

All that matters is that both of us are rapidly approaching that glowing blue disk, and a horrible frozen fate.

My feet pass through the disk, and I can feel the cold at once, working its way up my legs and numbing me to the bone. I gulp, closing my eyes so I don't have to watch my own doom.

Suddenly, a hand latches onto my flailing arm, gripping me tight and stopping me from going any farther.

Wardell? I glance up, expecting to see him.

Instead I see a winning smile combined with a kind of grimace. His concentration is complete as he hauls me back away from the disk by sheer strength, his other arm linked solidly through a rope that's tied around the nearby water fountain.

Tariq!

Keisha's scream cuts off, and I'm afraid I'll see her hurtling past me. There's no one left to save her since her cousin grabbed me instead. I risk a peek, and I see she's been caught, too! Her rescuer is wrapped in the

other end of the same rope, with its cords stretched tight across his wide body.

Wardell!

"Don't let go!" Tariq warns me, shouting to be heard over the noise the disk is making. It's like the sound of water rushing down a drain, only a hundred times louder.

"Don't worry, I won't!" I reply. I catch Wardell's eye, and he grins at me. Keisha's holding tight to his arm, which is around her in a bear hug. His bulk is good for this — she's not going anywhere.

The disk is down to the size of a large pizza. Now it's the size of a Frisbee. Now a DVD. Now a quarter. And then — pop! — it's gone. My feet hit the ground again. The rushing sound has diminished with it, and now it fades to nothing, leaving the hall quiet and still. No cold, no heat, no wind, no ice zombies. Nothing but the four of us and a rope.

We did it!

"It's over," I say softly, pulling free from Tariq and shaking off the last of the shivers and the cold. "Door's closed for good."

"Not just yet," Keisha corrects me, pushing her way out of Wardell's embrace and joining me in the middle of the hall. She holds up the ice ring, then drops it to the floor — and stomps on it. With each stomp her bejeweled high-top smashes it to tiny pieces. Each time the remnants flicker and then melt, leaving only a few stray droplets here and there. "Now it's over," she says, dusting off her hands. "Didn't want anybody trying that key again."

"No, we definitely don't," I agree. I turn to Tariq. "Thanks for the save, Tariq."

"No worries. We said we got this." He raises his fist, and I bump it with my own. Then he turns to Wardell and offers the same gesture. "Nice moves, dude."

Wardell's grin just gets wider. "Thanks. You, too." They bump fists, and I do believe Wardell stands straighter. He turns to look at Keisha, and she sighs, then shrugs.

"Yeah, whatever," she says finally. "Thanks for saving me and all." She doesn't offer her hand, but Wardell doesn't look too upset. Honestly, a thank-you from Keisha was probably a lot more than he or anyone was expecting.

"No problem," he says as casually as he can manage. He leans over and grabs his backpack from the floor. It looks like someone sprayed water on it. "We should probably get back."

Oh, right. Class. School. Normal stuff. I almost forgot. I follow Wardell as he retraces our steps toward the library. "Hey, where'd that rope come from?" I ask as we walk. "That was smart, tying it around the water fountain."

"Wardell's idea," Tariq tells me, nodding at my friend. "When the disk started pulling zombies back in, he figured you might need something to hold on to. We found it in the janitor's closet."

"Smart." I pat Wardell on the back. "Knew you had my back, Wardell."

"Always," he replies.

We get back to the library just as the bell rings. Maybe now everything can go back to normal!

12

Nothing to It

Oh. Right.

Mrs. Crump calls for lines, we trek back to class, and what's the first thing she does once we're all in our seats? She pulls a piece of paper off the bulletin board. A sign-up sheet, to be precise — one with only two names on it.

Gulp.

"Now, class," she announces, "as you know, each school year every grade gets to elect a hall monitor at Thurgood Cleavon Wilson Elementary. The job is open to any student who wants to apply for it. It's an important responsibility — the hall monitor makes sure no one is running or being loud or littering or bothering other students. The monitor makes sure no one gets lost, escorts visitors, and generally keeps our halls nice and clear and clean." She beams at Tariq, who smiles back but without his usual earth-shattering charm for a change. Almost like his heart's not in it this time.

"Your classmate Tariq has been hall monitor every year since first grade," Mrs. Crump continues, "and I hear he has done an excellent job of it." Keisha starts clapping, and the whole class follows suit. The thing is, Tariq really has been a good hall monitor. He likes being the center of attention. He wants everyone to look up to him. But I have to admit he doesn't mind doing the work to earn that kind of respect, either.

"This year, we have two students applying for the job!" Mrs. Crump sounds all excited about this. I'm pretty sure she's the only one. "We have Tariq, of course, but we have another of your classmates, Bakari Katari Johnson!" Ugh, right now hearing my full name like that just reminds me of Zenon. It gives me the shivers, though part of that might be just from remembering how cold his world was. Brrrr.

Mrs. Crump is still talking. "Since we have two candidates, I'm going to ask each of them to tell you a little about himself and why he'd make a good hall monitor. Then we'll put it to a vote. The student with the most votes gets the job. Does that sound fair?" Everyone nods.

This is my chance, and my hand shoots up before she can say anything else. "Mrs. Crump," I call out, "I'd really like to speak first, if that's all right."

The way she's looking at me, you'd think I'd grown a second set of arms. I haven't, have I? The way today's been going, I wouldn't be all that surprised. I guess it's unusual for me to volunteer to speak in front of the class.

I've never been comfortable talking in public. I nearly threw up in second grade when I had to deliver a line in our school play! But somehow, after ice zombies and everything else, it just doesn't seem all that scary anymore.

"Of course, Bakari," she tells me. "Go right ahead." That's what I like about Mrs. Crump. She tries to be fair to everybody.

I get up and walk to the front of the room. Everybody's watching me. Nobody's whispering or giggling or glaring. Not even Keisha. She's just sitting there quietly with the rest, waiting to hear what I have to say.

Too bad I have absolutely no idea.

"Thank you," I start out. That sounds like a good beginning. "I'm really glad to have this opportunity to apply for the job of hall monitor." Not too bad. I sound very businesslike. "The thing of it is —"

And that's where I draw a complete blank.

What do I want to tell them? I think desperately. I'm supposed to explain why I'd be a good hall monitor. Well, why would I? More importantly, why would I be a better hall monitor than Tariq?

Would I?

Then, in a flash, I know exactly what to say.

"The thing of it is," I continue, trying to act like I had this planned all along, "I don't think you should pick me as your hall monitor." There are a few gasps around the room. Some of the other kids sit up and look around like they fell asleep and are wondering if they're still dreaming. Keisha's frowning like she thinks this is some kind of trick. Wardell looks confused, but when my eyes meet his, he smiles and gives me a thumbs-up. At least I know I'd have gotten one vote.

But the truth is, it would've been the only one.

Even I would've voted for Tariq over me. He's just the better kid for the job.

And that's exactly what I tell them. "I'd like to be your hall monitor," I say, "but I got to watch Tariq in action today and he's really something. He's really there when you need him. He's exactly what a hall monitor should be. I don't think I could do the job half as well as he does, and Thurgood Cleavon Wilson Elementary's fourth-grade class deserves the best hall monitor it can have. That hall monitor is our own classmate, Tariq Thomas!"

I end by applauding Tariq, and Keisha quickly joins in. So does the rest of the class. Funny thing is, I get the feeling some of that clapping is for me, too.

"Well, Bakari, thank you for that inspiring speech," Mrs. Crump tells me as she steps up and gestures me back to my seat. "That was very well put, and it's refreshing to hear someone admit when they're not the best person for something. That takes honesty and a lot of self-knowledge." She smiles at me. It's the warmest, kindest smile I've ever seen from her.

"Tariq," she adds, turning to him, "since Bakari has withdrawn, the job of hall monitor is still yours. If you want to keep it, of course."

Tariq stands up. "Yes, ma'am," he tells her. "And I just want to say thank you to Bakari. I think he'd have been a better hall monitor than he says." He nods to me, and I

nod back. Maybe we're not worst enemies after all. Not today at least.

"Too bad, Bakari," someone says, and I look around to see Niecy nodding to me. "Maybe next time." She doesn't sound like she's making fun of me, either.

"Yeah, but cool speech," Raymond adds.

"Definitely," his best buddy Antwone agrees. "If we ever had two hall monitors, you'd totally get my vote!"

A few other kids say similar things. It's so weird. Before today, I wasn't sure any of them even knew my name! I am sure most of them have never talked to me before. Now here they are, acting like we're pals or something.

Part of me wonders if maybe they noticed more about today's events than I thought. Did they see me save them from those first two ice zombies during lunch? Do they know that me and Wardell and Keisha and Tariq saved all of them — and the rest of the world, too — from a total ice zombie invasion?

Or is it all about my little speech just now? This was the first time I spoke up, so I guess it makes sense that it's the first time any of them really listened to me. For a brief moment, I feel connected to the school, this class, and everyone in it. All this time I've always felt like I was all alone — well, except for Wardell. Now I actually feel like I belong. And I like it.

"That was awesome!" Wardell whispers to me as Mrs. Crump instructs everyone to take out their science books.

"Awesome?" I whisper back. "I withdrew from the race before it even got to a vote!"

"Yeah, but you stood up and did it," he replies. "You really stepped up, Bakari." He holds up his fist, and I bump it.

Yeah, I did, didn't I?

I glance up — and catch Keisha watching us. She obviously saw us whispering. Now's when she usually calls over Mrs. Crump to tell her we're not paying attention. But this time, she just half smiles at me. And gives me the tiniest of nods, a nod and a half smile she would totally deny if I ever mentioned it.

But I know it was there.

I smile back at her, and turn to the day's science lesson. But while I'm reading I slip a hand into my pocket and find Granddad's marble. "Light, courage, power," I tell it quietly. "You were right, Granddad. That's all you need."

I squeeze my eyes shut, then open them again. Shut, then open. Shut, then open.

You know, for a day that started off so terrible, it hasn't turned out too badly, after all.

Acknowledgments

Bakari and his friends would not be possible without my editor Andrea Davis Pinkney, and Marie Dutton Brown, my agent and my mentor. Then, too, the original clump, my dear cousins Wilton, Joseph, Willie, and Timothy. Shout-outs to the busy moms who lent an open ear and heart during this long journey: Monique, Mika, Robin, Ylonda, Annie D., Adaora, Andrea, Dr. Elena Jones, and Michelle E. Deep gratitude to my *Essence* family, past and present. Special thanks: Frank Acosta, Lynn Whitfield, Rhonda Joy McLean for the great recommendation, and to Dr. Thelma Baxter and Mr. Billy Baxter for the much-needed retreat. Shaun Robinson, you always make me smile. The late, great Daren Kerr, your spirit guides me still. And to all the courageous and patient dreamers everywhere (you know who you are).

About the Author and Illustrator

Patrik Henry Bass, editorial projects director at *Essence* magazine, is an award-winning journalist and frequent presence on radio and television. He has written for numerous publications, including the *New York Times*; *O, The Oprah Magazine*; the *Washington Post*; *Entertainment Weekly*; *Time Out New York*; and *Publishers Weekly*. A sought-after speaker and expert on popular culture and the arts, Bass has appeared on MSNBC, CNN, *The Steve Harvey Morning Show*, National Public Radio, *Access Hollywood*, Arise TV, BBC News, and is a contributor for *The Takeaway* on Public Radio International and WNBC-TV in New York City. A former professor at New York University's Department of Journalism, Bass is a proud Brooklynite.

Jerry Craft is the creator of *Mama's Boyz*, an award-winning comic strip that has been distributed by King Features Syndicate to almost nine hundred publications since 1995, making him one of the few syndicated African American cartoonists working today. He has illustrated and/or written several children's books, including *Hillary's Big Business Adventure*, *Looking to the Clouds for Daddy*, and *What's Below Your Tummy-Tum*. Most recently he has produced two chapter books: *Khalil's Way*, written by David Miller, and *Who Would Have Thunk It!*, written by George C. Fraser and Emma Fraser-Pendleton. He lives in Norwalk, Connecticut.